Cool Pets for Kids

Dogs

DAWN TITMUS

PowerKiDS
press

Published in 2019 by The Rosen
Publishing Group, Inc.
29 East 21st Street, New York, NY 10010

Cataloging-in-Publication Data

Names: Titmus, Dawn.
Title: Dogs / Dawn Titmus.
Description: New York : PowerKids Press, 2019. | Series: Cool pets for kids | Includes glossary and index.
Identifiers: LCCN ISBN 9781538338711 (pbk.) | ISBN 9781538338704 (library bound) |
ISBN 9781538338728 (6 pack)
Subjects: LCSH: Dogs--Juvenile literature. | Pets--Juvenile literature.
Classification: LCC SF426.5 T58 2019 | DDC 636.7--dc23

Text and editor: Dawn Titmus
Editorial Director: Lindsey Lowe
Children's Publisher: Anne O'Daly
Design Manager: Keith Davis
Picture Manager: Sophie Mortimer

Photo acknowledgements:
t=top, c=center, b=bottom, l=left, r=right
Interior: Alamy: blickwinkel/McPHOTO/WRO 18/19; iStock: andresr 8/9, baramee2554 7tr, Bigandt
Photography 27br, busypix 6br, cynoclub 3, 15br, 22/23, 24/25, 26/27; Fat Camera 5cl, Fenne 25tr, fotoedu
10/11, GlobalP 4/5, JPercha 7cl, Kali9 14br, 25br, LeslieLauren 29br, lleerogers 6bc, Maica 13tr, mauinow1
13br, mehmettoriak 7br, Deniz Murat 12/13, nimu1956 18bl, papound 7cr, vvvita 4cl, yellowsarah 1, 19br;
Shutterstock: Anneka 14/15, Bolt Photo 29tr, Casteco Design 28, cynoclub 11br, FabrikaSint 14bl, liike 17tr,
Jack Jelly 9tr, Budmin Jeutic 23br, kurashova 29bl, Dorottya Mathe 17bl, schubbel 16, Rin Seiko 23tr, Sladic
10br, Sundays Photography 27tl, Helen Sushitskaya 21tr, Tropical Studios 21br; Thinkstock: amactor 9tc,
GlobalP 20/21, Lucato 9c, malamooshi 12bl, Monkey Business Images 19tr, Padrin7 8cr.

Manufactured in the United States of America

CPSIA Compliance Information: Batch #CSPK18: For Further Information contact Rosen Publishing, New York,
New York at
1-800-237-9932.

Contents

Which Dog?

Dogs are popular pets and can bring a lifetime of happy memories. Dogs can be fun companions. All dogs need love, care, and attention, but some breeds are more demanding than others.

Your Home and Lifestyle

Before you choose a family dog, you need to think about how you live. Will the dog be alone during the day, or will someone be home to keep it company? Do you have a backyard or do you live in an apartment with no outside space? Some dogs get along well with other pets in the house. Others like to be the only pet. Dogs such as terriers are bred to chase small animals. They are more likely to run after cats!

Puppy or Older Dog?

Puppies need a lot of attention. You will have to housebreak a puppy and spend lots of time with it at first. You may find that an older dog is better suited to your family.

Rescue a Dog!

Rescue centers are full of dogs and puppies that need new homes. Check your local center to see if you can give a pet a forever home before you buy from a breeder.

The Right Dog For You?

☑ Will the dog have company during the day?

☑ Do you have the time to give an active dog lots of exercise every day?

☑ Can your family afford the food costs and vet bills?

☑ Do you have another pet in the home?

Read On ...

Dogs are great pets and make loyal companions, but it is important to choose the right one for you. This book will help you to pick and care for your pet. Learn about four of the most family-friendly breeds. Try your hand at making some tasty doggy cookies. You will also find some fascinating facts about your new best friend!

What You Will Need

All dogs need some basic items. They need food and water bowls, a collar and leash, and some toys. Your dog will also need a bed or crate to sleep in.

What You Need

- ☑ Food and water bowls the right size for your dog.

- ☑ Collar with ID tag and a leash.

- ☑ Grooming brushes and comb.

- ☑ Pooper-scooper and poop bags. The law says you must pick up after your pup!

- ☑ Toys, such as tug-of-war rope, chew toys, balls, and ball thrower.

- ☑ Bed or crate for sleeping.

Dog Bowls

Food and water bowls should be large enough for your dog to get its mouth inside easily. Nonslip bases on bowls are useful, so your pooch does not push its food around the floor!

Metal bowls do not break.

Grooming

All dogs need grooming—some more than others. You will need a brush and comb especially for your dog. A slicker brush has small pins on it. They are good for getting tangles out of hair. An ordinary bristle brush is good for giving the coat shine.

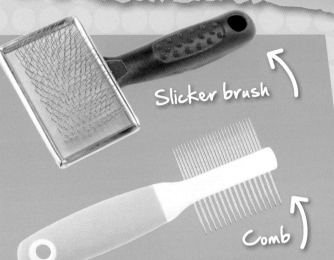

Slicker brush

Comb

Harnesses or Collars?

If a dog pulls on the leash, the collar can put pressure on its neck and cause injury. A harness can be a better way to keep control of your dog on walks. A harness can help stop a dog pulling on the leash. Make sure you fit the right size harness for your dog.

Microchips

A microchip is placed under your dog's skin. The chip has a number that identifies your dog. If your dog goes missing and is found by someone, animal control scans the chip to read the number.

Dog License

In most states, dogs must have a license. Attach an ID tag with the license number to your dog's collar. If your dog goes missing, a license tag helps animal control get your dog back to you quickly.

Feeding Time

Your dog needs the right amount of food to keep it fit and healthy. It also needs a supply of clean water. How much to feed your pooch depends on its size, age, and activity.

Tidbits and Treats

Rewarding good behavior with a tidbit or treat is a fun way for your dog to learn. You can buy treats specially for dogs in the store. Most dogs also like small pieces of cheese and cooked chicken. Be careful not to overfeed your dog with treats!

All types of chews are tasty treats.

How Much to Feed

The feeding guide on your dog's food label tells you how much to feed your dog, depending on its weight. Make sure you measure your dog's food. Ask an adult to check your dog's weight every two to three weeks. If your dog is gaining or losing weight, you'll need to adjust the amount of food or exercise it has.

Some people like to feed their dogs canned food. Other people prefer to give kibble (dried food). You can also feed your dog a mixture of both. Just be sure to give the right amounts for your dog's weight, age, and daily activity. Puppies need to be fed about three or more times a day. Adult dogs should eat one or two meals a day.

Kibble
(dried food)

Canned
meat meal

Complete
dried food

Poison!

Some foods are poisonous for dogs. Never feed your dog grapes, onions, avocados, rhubarb, fruits with pits such as peaches, or mushrooms. Chocolate can be poisonous, too. Baker's chocolate is more toxic than milk or white chocolate.

Grooming and Cleaning

Some dogs have thick, silky coats. Others have short, fluffy coats. Whatever breed your dog is, you need to groom it to remove dead hair. Almost all breeds molt twice every year. Some breeds do not molt, but they need to be groomed and clipped regularly.

Healthy Teeth

Just like people, dogs need to have clean, healthy teeth. Ask an adult to help you clean your dog's teeth. You will need special tasty toothpaste made for dogs—don't use ordinary toothpaste. You can use an old toothbrush or a finger brush. You may need to get your dog used to you handling its mouth at first. Pull up the dog's lips and brush the teeth gently. Work your way from front to back.

Bathtime

If you need to give your dog a bath, use a mild baby shampoo or a special shampoo for dogs. Make sure you rinse all the shampoo out with warm water. Have a dog towel ready for the big shake-off!

Getting Rid of Tangles

Use a comb or slicker brush to detangle your dog's coat. Comb out any dead hair from the undercoat. Then brush the coat, starting at the head and working toward the back. Gently brush your dog's chest and tummy area. Brush down the legs to the feet.

Ticks and Fleas

Ask an adult to help check and remove any ticks. Ticks carry diseases. If you see flea dirt—small, dark specks on the skin—ask an adult to give your dog some antiflea treatment.

Exercise

All dogs need exercise to stay healthy and in shape. Some breeds, such as the Border Collie, need lots of exercise. Others, such as the Great Dane, are happier on the sofa. Two to three walks a day will keep most dogs in shape.

Playtime

Lots of dogs love to play. Different breeds like different types of games and activities. Retrievers enjoy playing fetch games with a ball or favorite toy. Greyhounds like to run fast. Terriers were bred to find rats or foxes, so they often like sniffing and digging.

Puppies

Your puppy cannot be taken for a walk until it has had all its shots. Until then, you can carry it about in your arms to introduce it to noises and smells in the outside world.

Senior Dogs

As dogs age, they still need regular exercise. They might not walk as far as they used to, but they will enjoy going out. Walking will help prevent them from gaining weight and keep their joints mobile.

Off Leash

Dogs love being free to explore off the leash. They will travel three to four times farther than you do. Train your dog to come back when called. Only let your dog off the leash in a safe place away from traffic. Some city parks do not allow dogs to be off the leash.

Training

A well-trained dog is a pleasure to know. A poorly-trained dog can be a nuisance, even dangerous. Reward your dog when it gets things right. If training is fun, your dog will be more likely to learn what you want it to do.

Good Practice

Use a happy voice to tell your dog what you want it to do. Use the same words each time. Reward the behavior you want as soon as it happens. First reward small steps, such as moving in the right direction. Then reward the whole action, such as coming when called.

Rewards

You can use treats, toys, praise, or play as rewards for good behavior.

Housebreaking a Puppy

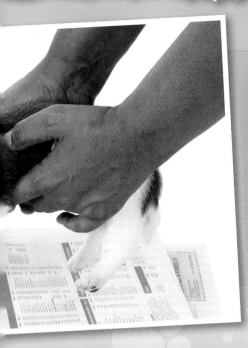

Learn the signs that your puppy wants to use the bathroom, such as walking in circles. Let the puppy outside and praise it when it uses the bathroom in the right place. Put down a sheet of newspaper if you live in an apartment. When the puppy has learned to use it, put the paper outside. Praise the puppy when it relieves itself outside.

Basic Commands

There are some basic commands all dogs should learn. These are coming when called, sit, lie down, walking on a loose leash, leave, and stay. When your dog has learned the basics, you can train it to do fun tricks such as shaking a paw.

Short Sessions

Keep your training sessions short. Practice for a few minutes each time, several times a day. Before long, you will have the best-trained pooch in the neigborhood!

Staying Healthy

You can help your dog stay healthy by making sure it gets enough exercise and its shots are up to date. Even so, just like people, dogs get sick sometimes.

Fleas and Worms

Make sure your pet is up to date with antiflea and worming treatments. Fleas can cause severe itching and allergies in your dog. Fleas can also pass on tapeworms. These parasites can cause illness if left untreated.

Coat and Skin

When you groom your dog, look out for rough or red patches of skin. Also check for bald or thinning patches on your dog's coat. If your dog starts to scratch itself more than usual, or chews its paws, take it to the vet. In most cases, the vet can treat your dog's skin and coat problems with medicine.

A Visit to the Vet

Take your dog to the vet once a year for its booster shots and a checkup. The vet will ask questions about your dog's general health and any problems it may have. Take along some treats so your dog has good memories of its visit to the vet.

Paw Problems

Check your dog's paws regularly for any problems. Look for cuts, scratches, thorns, or grass seeds. If your dog is constantly licking its paws, it may have an injury.

Shots

Puppies are usually vaccinated against disease when they are six to eight weeks old. They will need follow-up shots, and then booster shots every year to prevent disease.

In the Wild

People have bred dogs over thousands of years. Today, there are hundreds of different breeds. Although there is such a huge variety, all pet dogs are descended from wolves.

Wolf Pack

Wolves live in packs of at least two animals, usually more. Each wolf knows its place, or rank. The strong, or dominant, wolves are called alpha dogs. They get first choice on everything, including eating first and choosing where to sleep. Lower-ranking dogs treat them with respect.

Dingoes

Dingoes are semi-wild dogs that live in Australia. They live alone or in packs of up to 10 dogs. As with wolves, there are alpha dogs and pack rules.

The Family Pack

For your dog, your family is the pack. Your pet will pick up signals about who is in charge. It should be the lowest member of the pack. If a dog thinks it ranks high, there can be problems such as growling, snarling, or biting.

The Friendly Wolf

Most dog breeds do not look like wolves. Yet dogs' behavior and the way they communicate with each other are based on how wolves live. Think of your pet as a friendly wolf, and you'll understand each other just fine.

The Pack Rules

- ☑ Don't feed your dog tidbits from the table.

- ☑ Don't let it sit on furniture or sleep on your bed unless it is invited.

- ☑ Feed your dog at feeding time, not when it demands to be fed.

- ☑ Teach your dog to wait while you go first through doorways.

- ☑ Use clear instructions and reward your dog when it obeys them.

Labrador Retriever

The Labrador retriever, or Lab, is the most popular breed in the United States. It is friendly, affectionate, and intelligent, and makes an ideal family pet. Labs also make excellent "seeing eye" guide dogs for blind and partially sighted people.

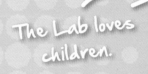

The Lab loves children.

Where in the World?

This loyal and reliable pooch comes from Newfoundland in Canada. The local fishermen used Labs to pull in their nets loaded with fish. Labs love water and go swimming any time they get the chance. They have a water-resistant coat, which keeps them warm.

Breed Profile

Labradors are strongly built. They are about 22 inches (56 cm) tall at the shoulder. The coat is short, straight, and thick. It comes in solid colors of black, yellow, or chocolate. Labs usually live 10 to 12 years.

Looking After Me

Labs are patient, reliable, and gentle. They are best suited to living in a family house with a yard.

☑ Labs enjoy family life, are gentle with children, and are easily trained.

☑ Labs need plenty of space and exercise. They are not suited to living in a small apartment.

Miniature Schnauzer

Active, lively, and friendly, the Miniature Schnauzer is the smallest of the schnauzer breeds. "Schnauze" is German for "muzzle." Farmers used these dogs to catch rats. They are also very keen guard dogs.

The Miniature Schnauzer is friendly and smart.

Where in the World?

The Miniature Schnauzer comes from Germany and was first bred in the mid- to late 1800s. It is a mix between the bigger standard schnauzer and smaller breeds such as the Affenpinscher.

Miniature Schnauzers stand about 12 to 14 inches (30 to 36 cm) at the shoulder. Their coat is short and wiry, and can be solid black, black and silver, or salt-and-pepper. They have very long whiskers and eyebrows. They live 12 to 14 years.

Looking After Me

The Miniature Schnauzer is a good family dog that enjoys company and family life.

☑ They make ideal companions for people who live in a city apartment, but they need plenty of activity to prevent boredom.

☑ The Miniature Schnauzer is a natural guard dog. It needs to be trained not to bark at visitors!

Shetland Sheepdog

Popularly known as the Sheltie, the Shetland Sheepdog was originally bred for herding sheep. Alert and intelligent, it is a popular family pet all over the world.

The Sheltie responds well to obedience training.

Where in the World?

The Shetland Sheepdog comes from the Shetland Islands, off the northern coast of Scotland. The thick coat of the Sheltie is well suited to the cold winter climate of these islands. The islands are also home to a miniature breed of pony.

Breed Profile

The Sheltie stands about 14 inches (36 cm) at the shoulder. It has thick white hair around the neck. The coat comes in different colors, including tan and white, and black and white. Shelties live 11 to 13 years.

Looking After Me

Shelties are loyal, affectionate dogs, and are gentle with children.

- ☑ They are often shy with strangers at first.

- ☑ Shelties are full of energy and need lots of exercise.

Jack Russell Terrier

A small, lively dog that loves long walks, the Jack Russell Terrier is one of the most popular breeds in the world. It is affectionate, fun loving, and friendly with children.

Where in the World?

The Jack Russell was first bred in England in the 1800s by the Reverend (Parson) Jack Russell. He liked fox hunting. The dog was trained to go down foxholes to chase out foxes. The dog had to run fast enough to keep up with the hunting horses.

Breed Profile

Jack Russells stand 10 to 14 inches (25 to 36 cm) at the shoulder. They have thick and smooth or wirehaired coats. The thick coat keeps the dog warm in cold weather. Jack Russells are usually white with black, lemon, or tan markings. They live 12 to 15 years.

Looking After Me

Very active and outgoing, Jack Russells need lots of exercise and training.

☑ They need to be occupied and should not be left alone for long periods. If they get bored, they will start chewing anything they can find.

☑ They can be noisy guard dogs, so will need to be trained to stop barking at your visitors!

The Jack Russell Terrier is a good family dog.

Make It!

Doggy Cookies

You can make these delicious cookie treats for your dog. Ask an adult to help when it's time to take the cookies out the oven. Your pooch will love them!

You Will Need:

3 cups (360 g) whole wheat flour

1 teaspoon garlic salt

½ cup (120 ml) soft bacon fat

1 cup (120 g) shredded cheese

1 egg, beaten slightly

1 cup (240 ml) milk

1 Ask an adult to help preheat the oven to 400°F (200°C/gas mark 6).

2 Put the flour and garlic salt in a large mixing bowl.

3 Stir in the bacon fat. Then add the cheese and egg.

4 Gradually add enough milk to form a dough.

5 Knead the dough and roll it out to about 1 inch (25 mm) thick.

6 Use a cookie cutter to cut out the dough or cut out shapes with a butter knife.

7 Place the dough pieces on a greased cookie sheet. Bake in a preheated oven for about 12 minutes, until they start to brown.

When they are cool, offer a cookie to your dog as a yummy treat!

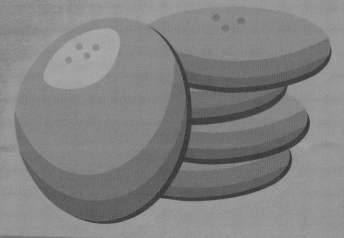

Did You Know?

The American Kennel Club (AKC) currently recognizes 202 dog breeds. The Fédération Cynologique Internationale (FCI) is the biggest dog organization in the world. It recognizes 332 breeds. That is the number of breeds that most kennel clubs worldwide recognize.

Dogs can hear sounds that are about four times farther away than humans can hear.

Dogs only have sweat glands in their paws. They have to pant to cool down on hot days. It can help to wet the pads of your dog's paws when it's hot.

The average dog can learn 165 words. In the US, a Border Collie named Chaser was trained to learn more than 1,000 words.

Some popular new breeds include Labradoodles, Yorkipoos, cockapoos, and schnoodles.

About 44 percent of all households in the United States have a dog. That adds up to about 78 million dogs in the US alone!

A dog's sense of smell is 10,000 to 100,000 times better than a human's. Some dogs have been trained to sniff out diseases such as cancer and diabetes in people.

Dogs have 42 teeth. That's 10 more than an adult human and 22 more than a child.

Glossary

breed (1) to take care of a group of animals to produce more animals of a particular kind. (2) a particular kind of animal that has been produced by breeding.

breeder person who breeds certain animals, such as dogs.

flea very small biting insect that lives on animals.

ID tag abbreviation of "identification" tag.

housebreak to train an animal to use the bathroom outside or in the correct place.

molt to lose hair and replace it with new growth.

parasite an animal that lives in or on another animal and gets food from it.

pooper-scooper device for picking up dog poop.

rank position in a group.

slicker brush brush with fine wire pins used for untangling hair.

smell receptor area in the nose that detects smells.

sweat gland area of the body that produces sweat.

tapeworm long, flat worm that lives in the stomachs of animals and people.

tick very small insect that attaches itself to a larger animal and feeds on it.

toxic poisonous or harmful.

undercoat a layer of short hair growing underneath the longer outer coat.

vaccination treatment with a substance, called a vaccine, to protect against a particular disease.

Further Resources

Books

O'Malley, Terry.
My First Dog: A Guide to Caring for Your New Best Friend, Create Space Independent Publishing Platform, 2016.

Pelar, Colleen.
Puppy Training for Kids: Teaching Children the Responsibilities and Joys of Puppy Care, Training, and Companionship, Barron's Educational Series, 2012.

Sundance, Kyra.
101 Dog Tricks, Kids Edition: Fun and Easy Activities, Games, and Crafts, Quarry Books, 2014.

Websites

Due to the changing nature of Internet links, PowerKids Press has developed an online list of websites related to the subject of this book. This site is updated regularly. Please use this link to access the list:

www.powerkidslinks.com/cpfk/dogs

Index